Howard B. Wigglebottom

Learns Too Much of a Good Thing is Bad

Howard Binkow

Susan F. Cornelison

Howard Binkow
Reverend Ana
Illustration by Susan F. Cornelison
Book design by Tobi S. Cunningham

Thunderbolt Publishing
We Do Listen Foundation
www.wedolisten.org

Gratitude and appreciation are given to all those who reviewed the story prior to publication.
The book became much better by incorporating several of their suggestions:

Karen Binkow, Erin Gaffny, Sherry Holland, Trish Jones, Renee Keeler, Lori Kotarba, Sarah Langner, Tracy Mastalski, Teri Poulus,
Laurie Sachs, Anne Shacklett, Mimi C. Savio, Karey Scholten, Nancey Silvers, Gayle Smith, Carrie Sutton, Rosemary Underwood,
and George Sachs Walor.

Teachers, librarians, counselors, and students at:

Blackbird Elementary, Harbor Springs, Michigan
Bossier Parish Schools, Bossier City, Louisiana
Central Elementary, Beaver Falls, Pennslyvania
Chalker Elementary, Kennesaw, Georgia
Charleston Elementary, Charleston, Arkansas
Forest Avenue Elementary, Hudson, Massachusetts
Golden West Elementary, Manteca, California

Iveland Elementary School, St. Louis, Missouri
Kincaid Elementary, Marietta, Georgia
Lamarque Elementary School, North Port, Florida
Lee Elementary, Los Alamitos, California
Prestonwood Elementary, Dallas, Texas
Sherman Oaks Elementary, Sherman Oaks, California
West Navarre Primary, Navarre, Florida

Printed in Malaysia by Tien Wah Press (PTE) Limited

Second printing September 2012

ISBN 978-09826165-3-6

This book belongs to

_____

4

"Happy birthday, Howard B. Wigglebottom!" shouted Uncle Joe as he brought in a big double-fudge chocolate brownie sundae.

5

YUM, Howard's favorite! It was seven in the morning and "I CAN'T HAVE TOO MUCH OF A GOOD THING," he thought. "It IS my birthday, after all, and I deserve a special breakfast!"

But after he
ate it all, his
tummy started
to rumble and
moan and groan.
"OH MY,"
said Howard.
He had no idea
something so
good could make
him feel so bad.

7

"Howard, it's time to get ready for school," his mother said. "Here are birthday treats to share with your friends after class."

Howard looked inside the bag. "Yum, bubblegum-my favorite! he said. "This is definitely a good thing!" as he popped one in his mouth.

One wasn't enough to even blow a baby bubble, so he decided two might be better–maybe many more. "CAN'T HAVE TOO MUCH OF A GOOD THING," he thought. Before long, Howard had stuffed the whole bag of bubble gum in his mouth.

He couldn't talk. His mouth was so full of gum that when the nicest girl in class asked if she could walk with him, all he could do was mumble "Ummmoummmmmeum," and no words came out.

"Oh, never mind," she said and walked away.

Howard walked by a balloon vendor on the way to school. How perfect, he thought. "It IS my birthday, after all, and I should have a balloon." He started to take one, then he thought: "One might be nice, maybe two, maybe many more. CAN'T HAVE TOO MUCH OF A GOOD THING."

When the man asked "How many?" Howard could only mumble, "Mummmmummmm."

Eighty-three balloons later . . .

. . . Howard's feet were no longer on the ground!

He was flying! "This is so cool!" Howard thought. "I'll let the breeze take me to school. That will be a good thing."

Just then, the little breeze became a big wind and carried Howard high over and way PAST his school.

He got a little worried. "How will I ever get back?" he wondered. "Oh, here comes a goose. Maybe he can help. That will be a good thing."

Oh my! There were hundreds of geese flying towards his balloons!!!

POP

18

POP

Howard was getting hot and tired. Then he felt a raindrop. "Oh, how nice! A little rain to cool me down," he thought. "That will be a good thing."

But it wasn't just a little
rain. Howard was in
the middle of a terrible
storm! He couldn't tell
the thunder from the
balloons popping all
around him. Howard
tried to yell for help
but his mouth was
so full of gum that
once again, only
"UMMMMUMUMUM"
came out.

POP

POP

POP

21

Then Howard looked down and saw his mom on a fire-truck ladder and lots of people. "Let go and land on the trampoline," shouted his mom. He was really scared. "Just do it!" everyone yelled.

Howard closed his eyes, counted to three and let go . . .

23

On the way down, Howard decided to practice a few flips. "One was good, two might be better, maybe many more. CAN'T HAVE TOO MUCH OF A GOOD THING," thought Howard.

Then . . . KERSPLAT! He landed on the trampoline. . .

But soon,
he found
himself in
his mother's
arms—
and that
definitely
was a very
good thing!!

Hours later, he was safe and warm at home. "I baked your favorite CARROT CAKE!" said his mom. "Because it's your birthday, you can have as many pieces as you like, watch TV and play games for as long as you wish tonight."

Howard thought . . . "Hmmm, maybe one, two, or maybe many more."

But Howard thought again.

Howard had learned his lesson for the day, after all. Too much of a good thing can turn into a BAD thing! "Mom," he said, "one piece of cake and one hour for TV and games will be enough, thank you."

"Good for you! Happy birthday, Howard!"

Howard B. Wigglebottom Learns Too Much of a Good Thing is Bad
Lessons and Reflections

★PLEASURE AND CONSEQUENCES

It's Very Hard to Stop Eating The Foods We Like.

Some foods, especially snacks and candy, smell and taste delicious. Our mouths water just thinking about them. We feel so good while eating them, we want to have more and more. We just can't stop eating–but then, just like what happened to Howard on page seven, we have a tummy ache and feel very bad.

Why is that?

It's because we forgot the "FOOD RULES." Our bodies don't like to have large amounts of foods, especially very sweet or very salty foods. Our bodies like just the right size and the right amount. It doesn't matter how good it looks or tastes.

So if we don't want to feel bad and hurt our bodies, we RESPECT THE FOOD RULES with just one piece of our favorite food at a time!

It's Very Hard To Stop Playing Games And Watching TV.

Playing games is fun! It feels good too, just like eating our favorite snacks and desserts. We want to do it more and more! It's so hard to stop.

We can play for hours, sometimes the whole day–but then we feel tired, cranky and unhappy. Our eyes become red and dry. Sometimes we can even get a headache and have problems sleeping.

Why is that?

It's because we forgot the "SCREEN RULES."

Children's bodies don't like to be in front of a screen–computer, video games, TV, etc.– for more than one hour at a time.

Whenever we don't follow these rules our bodies will feel bad. It doesn't matter how good the TV show or game is. If we spend too much time in front of a screen, there will be consequences; that means we will feel bad.

Don't let a good thing turn into a bad thing. Stop before it's too late!

★DISCIPLINE AND MODERATION

It's hard to say no to the foods and things we like. But if we want to grow up to be strong, healthy and powerful, we have to learn to follow the rules and stop before it is too late.

Just like everything else, it takes practice to be good at saying NO.

(Check out *Howard B. Wigglebottom Listens to His Heart* and *Howard B. Wigglebottom Learns It's OK to Back Away.*)

The more we practice, the better we get. Every time we stop eating or playing before we really want to, we will have a different kind of feeling good; it will feel like we won something really big.

Before you know it, you will be ready to be like all the people you admire; people who are very good following the rules and saying NO: Astronauts, Olympic champions, great soccer, baseball or football players, good doctors, firemen, presidents or who knows? Super heroes!

Learn more about Howard's other adventures.

BOOKS

Howard B. Wigglebottom Learns to Listen

Howard B. Wigglebottom Listens to His Heart

Howard B. Wigglebottom Learns About Bullies

Howard B. Wigglebottom Learns About Mud and Rainbows

Howard B. Wigglebottom Learns It's OK to Back Away

Howard B. Wigglebottom and the Monkey on His Back: A Tale About Telling the Truth

Howard B. Wigglebottom and the Power of Giving: A Christmas Story

Howard B. Wigglebottom Blends in Like Chameleons: A Fable About Belonging

Howard B. Wigglebottom Learns About Sportmanship: Winning Isn't Everything

WEBSITE

Visit www.wedolisten.org

- Enjoy free animated books, games, and songs.
- Print lessons and posters from the books.
- Email the author.